STINKY'S STORIES
THE BOY WHO CRIED
UNDERPANTS!

Read more Stinky's Stories!

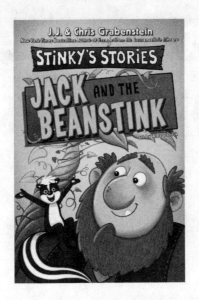

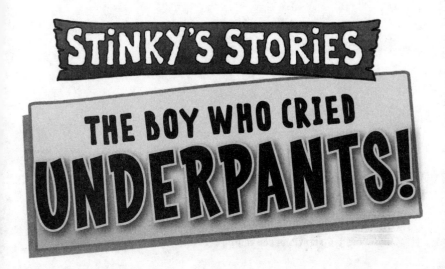

New York Times Bestselling Author
Chris & J.J. Grabenstein

art by Alex Patrick

HARPER
An Imprint of HarperCollinsPublishers

CONTENTS

CHAPTER ONE

STORY TIME!

Hi there!

I'm Stinky. Yeah, that's my name. Probably because I'm a skunk. Aren't you glad this isn't a "scratch 'n' sniff" book?

That lady reading the story to the kids? That's Mrs. Emerson. She's the school librarian. She's also the nicest person in the whole building.

Today, Mrs. Emerson read a story from the *Big Book of Fables*. She even did voices!

"'The shepherd boy cried, "Wolf! Wolf!"'" she read.

Of course, I already knew the whole story. I've heard it a million times. It's what they call a classic. That means it's old.

"The Boy Who Cried Wolf" was written more than two thousand years ago by a guy named Aesop. He wrote a bunch of famous fables, like that one about the tortoise and the hare. I don't have hair. Not real hair, at least. I'm a stuffed animal. My fur is soft, plush fuzz.

Mrs. Emerson turned the page. "'The

angry villagers charged up the hill with pitchforks. They were ready to chase off the wolf.'"

"Uhhhhh-ohhhhh," Geri the giraffe whispered. "They're gonna poke that wolf in the buh-utt!"

Geri is an odd giraffe. You might notice that she's sitting on a lower shelf, next to Wags the dog and Mr. Stuffington the bear. I live on the top shelf because—you guessed it—I'm Mrs. Emerson's favorite.

"'The shepherd boy saw all the villagers running around with their pitchforks and looking for the wolf,'" said Mrs. Emerson. "'He doubled over with laughter. He had only pretended there was a wolf. He thought the trick he played was very funny.'"

"That's the third time the boy cried 'wolf,'" said Geri. "I've been keeping score."

"This story is preposterous." Mr. Stuffington sniffed.

"There's a rhinoceros?" Geri asked.

"No, Geri!" Mr. Stuffington explained. "I said it's 'preposterous.' That means it's silly! Why would any village put a young boy in charge of sheep security?"

"Shhh!" said Wags. "I want to hear what happens next!"

CHAPTER TWO

WHO'S AFRAID OF THE BIG BAD WOLF?

"'The very next day,'" said Mrs. Emerson, "'a big bad wolf really did spring out of the woods.'"

All the kids on the story rug gasped when Mrs. Emerson read that bit. I told you. She's good.

Mrs. Emerson continued reading. "'The boy shouted "Wolf! Wolf!" But the villagers thought he was trying to trick them again. So they didn't come to help.

"'At sunset, the shepherd boy still hadn't returned to the village. A wise old man went looking for him. He found the boy weeping in the empty meadow.

"'"There really was a wolf this time!" said the boy. "Why didn't anybody help me?"

"'The old man told the boy these very wise words. . . .'" Mrs. Emerson put on her creaky, old-man voice. "'"Nobody believes a liar. Even when he is telling the truth."'"

Mrs. Emerson closed the book. "The end."

"Were the sheep okay?" asked Abby, a

very shy third grader. Her eyes were wider than Wags the dog's.

"Oh, yes," said Mrs. Emerson. "The sheep were fine, just fine."

"But what happened to them that made the shepherd boy so sad?" asked Justus. He looked worried, too.

"What do *you* think happened?" said Mrs. Emerson. "Sometimes you have to use your imagination to find the ending you're looking for."

She stood up and had a big grin on her face.

"Now, if you children will excuse me, I must go shelve some returns."

She gave me a quick wink and walked away.

"I'm worried about the sheep," mumbled Abby after Mrs. Emerson was gone.

"Me, too," said Justus and his friend Mateo.

Abby looked up at me with tears in her eyes.

"I don't want the story to end that way, Stinky!" Abby whispered.

"Me neither," said Mateo.

The other kids nodded. Everybody wanted a different ending.

Yep. I had work to do.

This feels like a good time to tell you that, yes, the kids at Hickleberry Elementary can talk to us stuffies and we can talk to them. Not all the time, mind you. Only when there aren't any grownups nearby. Those are the rules. The kids all know to never tell anybody our secret. That would ruin the magic for everybody.

"Well," I told the class, "it's like Mrs. Emerson said—the story doesn't have to end that way. Not if we use our imaginations!"

CHAPTER THREE

A NEW TWIST

"I will now tell you what happened next," I told the kids.

"No, you will not," said Mr. Stuffington. (He can be very stuffy.) "Mrs. Emerson said, 'The End.' That means this story is over. We cannot rewrite the ending."

"We're not changing the ending. We're just adding to it," I said. "To do that, we just have to use our imaginations."

"Go on, Stinky!" barked Wags. "Tell us what happened next!"

"Please?" said Abby. "I'm really worried about the sheep."

"The sheep were fine," I told her. "When they saw the wolf coming, they rolled around in the grass and got all grass-stained. It turned out to be the perfect disguise. The wolf thought they were fluffy shrubs."

"Phew," said Abby. "I was so worried."

"But what about the boy who cried 'wolf'?" asked Wags.

"Oh, you mean Bob," I said. "Well, Bob's problem was he got very bored very easily."

"Is that why he cried 'wolf' when there wasn't really a wolf?" asked Geri.

"Yep," I explained. "And the very next day Bob was back on the hill with the green sheep. Grass stains don't wash out of wool very easily. You need mild soap and a lint-free cloth."

"What kind of story is this?" demanded Mr. Stuffington. "Why is there laundry in it?"

I ignored him. Trust me—it's better that way.

"Soon, Bob got bored again," I told the kids. "So he decided to play with his sheepdog, Molly."

"Oh boy, oh boy, oh boy," said Wags. "There's a dog in this story. I love stories with dogs in 'em."

Mr. Stuffington gave that an eye roll. "Of course you do."

"Bob got down on all fours," I said, "and shouted 'Woof!' Molly wagged her tail. So Bob did it again. 'Woof!' he cried. 'Woof!' His cries grew louder and louder. 'WOOF, WOOF, WOOF!'"

"Uh-oh," said Geri. "'Woof' sounds a lot like 'wolf.'"

The kids all nodded in agreement.

"That's right," I told them. "The boy who cried 'wolf' became the boy who cried 'woof.' And since several of the villagers had waxy buildup in their ears, they thought he was crying 'wolf' again."

"I was afraid something like this might happen," said Geri.

"The wise old man from the village was certain that Bob had learned his lesson. No way would Bob cry wolf again unless he really saw one. So the wise old man told all the other villagers to grab their pitchforks."

"Oh, no," said Wags.

"Oh, yes," I said. "They rushed up the hill only to find Bob rolling around on the

ground with Molly."

"Poor dog," said Wags. "She needs to hear more stories. Stories can help you learn new words."

"So, Bob lost his job?" asked Geri.

I nodded. "The village elders of Doonferbleck—"

"Wait one minute," said Mr. Stuffington.

"That's the name of the village? What kind of name is Doonferbleck?"

I, once again, ignored him.

"The village elders gave Bob a new job," I explained. "The easiest one they could find. It was also the most boring job in all the land."

"What was it?" asked Geri.

"Bob had to stand guard at the newly painted village sign and make sure the paint dried properly."

"He had to watch paint dry?" said Wags.

"Sheesh," said Geri. "That's duller than a mashed-potato sandwich."

"Yes," I said. "It was as dull as dishwater in a ditch, which is actually ditchwater. But there, by the side of the road, just at the entrance to the village was another sign."

The kids clapped their hands together.

"And what, pray tell, did *that* sign say?" asked Mr. Stuffington.

I smiled. "This Way to the Big City!"

CHAPTER FOUR

DOONFERBLECK

"Did he go?" asked Wags. "Did he, Stinky? Did he, did he, did he?"

"Not right away," I told him. "He was scared. The village of Doonferbleck was the only place Bob had ever lived."

"What a terrible name," said Geri.

"Bob?" said Mr. Stuffington. "I believe it is short for Robert."

"I mean Doonferbleck!" Geri explained. "Why was the village called that?"

"Easy," I told her. "Because of how their doonfer tasted."

"What's doonfer?" asked Geri.

"A type of mushy gruel. It's like oat-meal. Except doonfer is made with mashed beans, barley, bugs, and boogers."

"I'd eat it," said Wags, panting.

"Doonferbleck's doonfer was disgust-ing," I said. "Everyone who ever tasted it said 'bleck!' And so the name Doonfer-bleck stuck like the clumps of their doonfer to the roofs of so many mouths."

"That's the worst origin story I have ever heard," said Mr. Stuffington. "Somebody should really talk to their mayor."

"Anyway," I continued, "despite the terrible food, Bob didn't want to leave his home. Or his sheep. Or his dog, Molly. But that sign! The city seemed to promise so much."

"Cities can be quite exciting," said Mr. Stuffington. "Why, I remember when I was in London, on sale at a souvenir shop where Mrs. Emerson happened upon—"

"Let Stinky tell the story," said Wags. "I like Stinky's story better."

"Of course you do." Mr. Stuffington sniffed. "It has a dog in it."

"Suddenly," I said (because every story can use a good "suddenly"), "Bob had a very scary thought. *What if the city is full of wolves? What if wolves are all that lives there?*"

The kids gasped again.

"Wait a second," said Wags. "Not all wolves are big or bad. Just the big bad ones."

"What did Bob do?" asked Geri. "I can't stand the suspense!"

"Bob didn't know if he should stay or if he should go. That's when a little bird landed on the sign!"

"Did it need a place to poop?" asked Wags.

"Is this another plot twist?" asked Mr. Stuffington.

"Yes!" I said.

"How many twists are there going to be? Is this a story or a pretzel?" Mr. Stuffington complained.

"What did the little bird tell Bob?" asked Wags. "We need to know. We need to know right now!"

CHAPTER FIVE

A WORD FROM A BIRD

I puffed out my chest so I looked more like a bird. I made my voice warbly, too.

To do well in the big city, you must do one thing.

WELCOME TO
DOONFERBLECK
POPULATION
PEOPLE-130
SHEEP-502

What?

Sssssttttrrrreeeettttccchhhhh yyyyyoooouuuurrrrr iiiimmmaaaaggggiiiinnnnaaaattttiiiioooonnnn!

"Huh?" said Wags. "What language is that bird speaking? Sparrow?"

"I know what the bird is saying!" said Abby. "The bird is telling Bob to stretch his imagination! That's why the bird stretched out the word 'imagination'!"

"Exactly," I told her.

"It was like a puzzle!" said Abby. "I like solving puzzles."

"This is an inter-active story now?" mumbled Mr. Stuffington. "Please pick a lane, people."

"So," I said, "Bob set off for the big city. The sun shone brightly through the tree-tops. Bees buzzed. The air smelled fresh and clean. Which, I guess, is great if you like that sort of thing. We skunks? Not so much."

"Oh, get on with it," huffed Mr. Stuffington.

"Bob was so excited to start his new life that he didn't realize how far he'd walked. Off in the distance, he heard a voice."

"Who was it?" asked Wags. "Huh? Huh?"

"Bob couldn't tell. But as he moved closer, the voice became clearer. It was a man and he was shouting."

"What was he shouting?" Geri asked.

"Just one word," I explained.

"What was it?" said Wags. "What? What? What?"

I paused for just a second—and then I told them. "WOLF!"

CHAPTER SIX

THE MAN WHO CRIED WOLFE

"Wolf?" said Geri. "Isn't that the word that got Bob in trouble in the first place?"

"It sure is," I said. "He thought it might get him in trouble again. So he thought about turning around, going back home to Doonferbleck. But then he saw a flashing neon sign welcoming him to 'Wolfesburgh, Home of The William D. Wolfe Company, Makers Of All Sorts Of Fine And Fancy Stuff.'"

"There was room on the sign for all of that?" grumbled Mr. Stuffington. "How much electricity did that sign use every day?"

"A lot. Especially since Mr. Wolfe had an extra letter at the end of his name. It was spelled W-O-L-F-E!"

"So wasteful," Mr. Stuffington said. "Adding that useless extra e to a perfectly good word."

I ignored my friend again. "As it turns out, the first person Bob met at the city gates was the official town crier."

"That person must've been very, very sad," said Geri.

"I never cry," said Mr. Stuffington proudly.

"That's because your eyeballs are made of plastic!" said Geri.

"Quiet, guys," said Wags. "Let Stinky tell his story."

"Thank you." I cleared my throat and

continued. "In olden times a town crier was someone who made public announcements. But this particular town crier also wept a lot. Tears squirted out of his eyes as if they were lawn sprinklers.

"Yes," I told the kids, "the town crier was very good at his job. He could boo-hoo and blubber to beat the best."

Geri the giraffe raised a hoof. "Was there a town laugher, too?"

I shook my head. "No, Geri. But, suddenly, off in the distance, Bob heard more people crying 'Wolfe.' The town crier explained that people shouting Wolfe was how Mr. Wolfe advertised all of his Wolfe brand products. When Bob tried to thank the town crier for explaining, the man just blubbered louder and shouted 'Wolfe' in Bob's face.

Waa-Waa-waa-Wolfe

Why are you crying 'wolf'?

Because Mr. Wolfe pays people all over the city to shout his name.

Waa-Waa-Waa-Wolfe

"So," I said, "Bob slumped his shoulders and headed up the road toward the city center. The town crier hadn't been very friendly. Bob wondered if he'd made a mistake coming to the Big City.

"Would he ever find a friend? Fortunately, that's when Bob met . . . ME!"

Waa-waa-Waa-Wolfe

CHAPTER SEVEN

MY FAVORITE CHARACTER

"Wait a second," said Mr. Stuffington. "*You*, Stinky the Skunk, are now in this story?"

"Yep," I told him.

"I thought this was an ancient fable," muttered Geri.

"Nope. It's a Stinky story."

"You mean it's no good?" said Wags.

I flipped up my tail. "What do you guys want? My tale or my tail? I feel a rump rumble coming on."

All the kids giggled.

Mr. Stuffington scrunched up his nose. "Your tale. The story. Please."

"Very well. I was standing under a big video billboard. It was just up the road from the city's neon Welcome sign. First, the sign behind me was advertising Wolfe Brand Toothpaste-Filled Cupcakes. You brush your teeth with every bite. They had red frosting. So I made my rear end smell like raspberries."

"You did?" said Geri. "How?"

"It's a story. I can do anything. Suddenly, the sign changed to an ad for the Battery-Powered Wolfe Banana Zipper. If you only eat part of your banana, it zips the peel shut so you can finish it later. Now my butt smelled like banana bread. The sign changed again. This time it showed a baby crawling across the floor with sponges strapped to its hands and knees. It was an ad for the Wolfe Brand Baby Mop. Why just crawl across the floor when you can scrub it? By the way, I do an awesome dirty diaper. You guys want to smell it?"

"No!" the whole class shouted together.

"Bob told me how he used to cry 'wolf' back home in his village. I almost lost my lunch when he told me he came from Doonferbleck, because I've tasted their doonfer."

"You did?" said Geri.

"Oh, yes," I told her. "It smelled like I do ten minutes after I eat a beanie weenie burrito. Tasted horrible, too."

"There are boogers in it," said Geri, who had been paying very close attention

to all the details in my story.

"I know," I said. "Unfortunately, I thought they were raisins."

"Bleck!" said all the kids.

I nodded. "Very bleck, indeed."

CHAPTER EIGHT

A NEW JOB FOR BOB

When everybody stopped urping, I continued my tale.

"Bob told me his whole sad story. How he had cried 'wolf' when there wasn't a wolf. How the villagers of Doonferbleck didn't like that. I could relate. Nobody liked it that one time I let out a super gassy blast in a crowded movie theater. But I also realized that Bob had great experience crying 'Wolfe,' even if he'd only done it without the e. He'd be perfect for a job crying 'Wolfe' for Mr. Wolfe!

"And so," I said, "Bob and I hurried across town. People moved out of our way. Some even leaped off the sidewalk. They could smell us coming. Well, mostly they could smell me. Although Bob was also working up quite a sweat.

"When we got to the Wolfe Company's office building, Bob tilted back his head and gawked up at the shimmering glass tower. It was so tall it disappeared into the clouds. Mr. Wolfe's office was on the two-hundred-and-fifty-second floor. We'd need to take the elevator. I knew Mr. Wolfe would meet with us. His door was always open. Especially when I was around. He usually opened a few windows then, too.

"When we got there, Mr. Wolfe was tinkering on a new idea for a product:

Grass-Topped Flip-
Flops. When you
wore them, you would
have the toe-tickling feel-
ing of walking on grass
even when you were walking on con-
crete. I introduced Bob. I said he was a
boy who really knew how to cry 'Wolfe.'

Mr. Wolfe was thrilled to meet Bob and hired him on the spot."

"Really?" Mr. Stuffington sniffed. "He didn't ask for a résumé or references?"

"Nope," I said. "Mr. Wolfe needed lots and lots of people to cry 'Wolfe' for him. It was the only advertising he could do. Sure, he'd wanted to sing a jingle about his marvelous merchandise, but nothing rhymes with Wolfe. It's like orange. Or walrus."

"Oh, boy," said Wags, clapping his front paws. "Bob has a job! Bob has a job!"

"Soon, Bob was crying 'Wolfe' all over town. But after a month of repeating the same word over and over and over again, something happened to Bob. Something that had happened to him before."

"I bet he got bored," said Geri.

"Exactly!"

"So what did Bob do?" asked Wags.

"Well, being a very smart boy, he went looking for me!"

CHAPTER NINE

BOB'S BIG IDEA

"Did Bob find you?" asked Wags. "Did he? Did he?"

"Oh, yes," I said. "I'm pretty easy to find. You just have to follow your nose.

"Bob told me that he was super bored. In fact, he said he was bored to tears. I figured that was why the town crier wept all the time. He was probably bored to tears, too! Anyway, I asked Bob what he liked to do, more than anything in the world."

"I like to try on new vests," said Mr. Stuffington. "The more plaid, the better."

"I like when Abby and Mateo rub my floppy ears," said Wags.

"Me?" I said. "I like to make up new stinks. Like stinky cheese inside even stinkier gym socks."

"But what did Bob love to do?" asked Geri.

"Well," I said, "Bob liked to make things up, too. Not stinky smells. But other stuff. When he cried 'wolf' in that sheep meadow, there wasn't a real wolf, just the one he dreamed up in his head."

"He was using his imagination!" exclaimed Wags.

"Exactly! So I told Bob to do more of that. To see things that weren't there and make other people see them, too. I told him to use his imagination because his imagination could take him anywhere!"

"And did Bob listen to you?" asked Wags.

"Oh, yes. In fact, he might've listened a little too well. The very next day, all the other Wolfe criers were out and about. Some cried 'Wolfe!' in a high-pitched voice. Some cried 'Wolfe!' in a voice so deep it rattled windows. Some sang the word. Some shrieked it. The people in the city were so used to hearing the Wolfe criers, very few paid any attention to all the Wolfe-crying around them. But Bob soon found a way to attract everybody's attention."

"Did he rap?" asked Geri.

I shook my head. "Nope."

"Did he dance?" asked Wags.

"Bob couldn't dance. He had two left feet."

"Must have made it difficult for him to buy shoes," said Mr. Stuffington.

"So what did Bob do?" asked Wags. "Huh, huh? What was his big idea?"

"Bob decided to cry a new word," I said. "One that would surely grab everyone's attention."

"What was it?" wondered Geri.

And that's when I told them Bob's secret favorite word:

CHAPTER TEN

STINKY UNDERPANTS

"Yes," I told the class, "when Bob cried 'underpants,' everyone paid attention!

Oh, my! Can you really see my underpants?

Look, Stinky. Underpants.

You can see my stinky underpants? Yipes!

"The man tugged up on his belt loops and dashed off. Bob was laughing so hard, he had tears streaming down his cheeks. A lady walked down the sidewalk. Bob shouted 'UNDERPANTS' at her, too. She spun around. She sniffed the air. It smelled like me. So she thought she had stinky underpants. She yelped and ran away."

I lowered my eyes in shame. "I suppose it was all my fault," I said. "I was the one who told Bob that his imagination could take him anywhere.

I just pretend that I see their underpants and they think I can see their underpants! I'm using my imagination!

But was this really where he wanted to go? Bob even pointed at me and shouted 'UNDERPANTS.' I reminded him that I am a skunk. I don't wear underpants. I don't even wear pants-pants. I also didn't think crying 'underpants' at strangers was the best thing Bob could be doing with his talents. And you know what? I wasn't the only one who thought that."

"Uh-oh," said Geri. "Sounds like Bob's in trouble again!"

CHAPTER ELEVEN

THE POLITENESS POLICE

All the kids on the library story rug were shaking their heads.

"So did Bob quit crying 'underpants'?" said Abby.

"Did he?" asked Mateo.

"Yes," I told them. "But only because the politeness police came along and told him he had to.

What you are doing, dear boy, is very impolite.

It's also crude and rude.

"And so," I said, "Bob promised not to cry 'underpants' anymore.

"The officers let him off with a warning. They handed him a bright orange card with the word 'warning' printed on it. When Mr. Wolfe saw that warning card, Bob lost his job crying 'Wolfe.'"

"Poor kid," said Wags.

"Stuff and rubbish," said Mr. Stuffington. "The boy got what he deserved."

"Anyway," I said, "I tried to cheer Bob up. I told him he would find a new job soon. But with nothing fun or funny to cry and no mischief to make, Bob grew bored again. As the days dragged on, he thought about returning to Doonferbleck. But that would mean he'd be going home a loser. They'd probably give him an even worse job than watching paint dry. Like watching the grass grow."

"And," said Geri, "he'd have to eat mashed boogers for breakfast again."

I nodded. "Not knowing what to do or where to go, Bob somehow ended up in the city's biggest church. A grand cathedral with stained-glass windows, a towering ceiling, and a pipe organ. It was a Sunday. The pews were packed. A man in robes stood at the front with his arms open wide.

"And Bob got a horrible, terrible, unbelievably bad idea."

"What was it this time?" asked Mr. Stuffington.

"Bob was going to point at the man in robes and cry 'underpants,'" I said. "He thought it would be hysterical! A thousand people packed inside the church would all gasp at the same time. He thought it would be SO MUCH FUN!

"He was ready to spring into action," I said. "Fortunately, that's when I snuck into the church. I slipped through legs and under pews. I reached Bob's row and explained to him that this was not the time or place to cry 'underpants.' No matter how funny it might be.

"And Bob knew I was right. So, to distract himself, while the choir sang a hymn, Bob mumbled a song to himself. It sounded a lot like 'God Bless America.'"

"Do you remember the words

to the song?" asked Mr. Stuffington, because he always likes a jolly sing-along.

"Yes," I told him. Then, I recited a verse:

"God bless my underwear,
my only pair.
Stand beside them
and guide them,
as they sit in a heap by the chair.
From the washer to the dryer,
I just hope that they don't tear.
God bless my underwear. My butt's not bare."

"That is a very silly song." Mr. Stuffington sniffed.

"Hey, Stuffington," said Wags, "what are you doing under there?"

"Under where?"

Wags laughed. "Ha! I made you say 'underwear'!"

"And that song made Bob laugh," I said. "He didn't need to cry 'underpants'! I breathed a huge sigh of relief. But that's when the queen and all her ladies-in-waiting marched into the cathedral!"

CHAPTER TWELVE
HERE COMES THE QUEEN

I hopped off the shelf and paraded back and forth in front of the kids.

"Trumpets sounded," I told them. "The queen and all her court strode down the center aisle. I tucked in my tail so she wouldn't step on it. I didn't want her feet to smell worse than they already did. It's well known that all queens have very stinky feet. Too many glass slippers. Makes their toes sweat.

"The queen gave everybody a backward wave of her hand. It looked like she was changing a light bulb.

"The man in robes at the front of the cathedral swirled one hand grandly in front of his face and dipped into a deep bow.

"When he did that, everybody in the pews stood up except Bob. Bob wasn't used to being in the audience with a queen. So, from where Bob was sitting, he had a perfect, Bob's-eye view of what happened next."

Helloooooooo, little people. Helloooooo!

"What was that?" asked Wags.

"Well," I said, "the day before, there had been a huge feast day. Everybody's clothes were extra tight. When they bent over to bow, pants split, skirts ripped, and zippers unzipped. Bob's eyes were right at bum level. Bob saw everyone's underpants. Lots and lots of underpants. Red underpants. Green underpants. Purple polka-dot and pink paisley underpants. Most of the underpants were clean, but some underpants were saggy and droopy. Bob saw them all, and he knew exactly what he had to do."

"He's going to cry 'underpants' again, isn't he?" guessed Mr. Stuffington.

"Yep! He felt it was his duty. Someone needed to warn these people that their underwear was showing!

"Bob leaped to his feet and cried 'underpants' at the top of his lungs! He pointed left, he pointed right, he pointed sideways. 'Underpants! Underpants! Underpants!' He was surrounded by pantaloons playing peekaboo through slits and slashes and rips and gashes.

"Everyone in the church gasped. Bob didn't know it, but it was against several different royal decrees for anybody to talk about undergarments when the queen was in the room."

"What'd the queen do, Stinky?" asked Wags. "Huh? What'd she do?"

"She told her subjects that she was not amused. And then she asked who would dare cry that foul word so loudly in her presence. Bob, of course, was terrified, but he knew he had to tell the truth.

"I knew I had to do something to save Bob! Fast! So I scooted next to Bob's ankle, flipped up my tail, and let 'er rip. I pumped a gassy blast out of my tailpipe. It smelled like sewer sludge that had been sitting in the sun!

"The queen nearly fainted. She thought my stench was coming from Bob. She worried that Bob would make her dungeon stink worse than it already did. The queen immediately issued a new decree. The stinky country boy who dared cry 'underpants' in her presence would be sent home. He would be carted back to Doonferbleck."

Geri shook her head. "Poor Bob. He's going back to booger town."

CHAPTER THIRTEEN

HOME, BLECK HOME

"And so," I continued, "Bob was put on the next donkey cart home to Doonferbleck."

"All because he tried to warn people that their underwear was showing?" said Mr. Stuffington. I could tell. He had grown to like Bob. "They should have declared him a hero and given him a parade."

"I love parades," said Geri.

"Me, too," said Wags. "Hey, Stinky? Can this story have a parade in it?"

"Not right now," I told him. "First,

Bob must go home in disgrace for crying 'underpants.'"

"But it needed to be done!" said Mr. Stuffington. "Their underwear was exposed!"

"What happened next, Stinky?" asked Geri.

"Well," I said, "when the donkey cart dropped Bob off in the village square, he knew he needed a job. So he went to the town elders to see what he could do.

"A wise old man told Bob that they had just the job for him. They needed someone to count all the strands of hay in all the haystacks. Any knitting needles he found he could keep.

"Bob thanked the elders. It wasn't exactly his dream job, but he felt lucky to have something to do. Bob spent day after day counting hay. As he counted, his mind

wandered. He thought about his life in the big city. He swore to himself that, if he ever got a second chance, he'd use his imagination to come up with something that could help other people."

"Poor guy," said Wags.

Mr. Stuffington sniffled and dabbed at his eyes. "Poor, poor Bob."

"Is this how the story ends?" asked Geri. "I like happy endings!"

"Well, you're in luck," I said. "For, at that very moment, Bob heard a voice. Someone calling to him from across the hayfield!"

"That's you, right, Stinky?" said Wags.

They need you, Bob! They need someone to tell them a truth they can't see for themselves!

"You're back in the story?"

"Yes, I am. I went searching for Bob because I knew the city needed Bob's special talents."

"Counting straw?" said Geri.

"No. The kids of the city needed Bob to cry 'underpants' again!"

CHAPTER FOURTEEN

THE UNDERPANTS AVENGER

I leaped up to my spot at the top of the bookcase.

"I told Bob how bad things were in the city. How showing your underwear now meant showing the queen how much you loved her!

"In fact, the first thing most grown-ups in the city did when they bought new clothes was to rip a hole in the seat of their pants or skirt."

"Because it showed the queen how deeply they bowed?" asked Geri.

"Exactly! And, oh, were the city children miserable with this new fashion trend. Children see the world at butt level. They were looking at grown-ups' underwear all day long. They needed Bob to come back and save the day!"

"What'd you guys do?" asked Wags. "Huh, huh?"

"Bob hatched a clever plan," I said, rubbing my paws together eagerly. "He'd get all the other children to cry 'underpants' with him! Why, they'd be so loud, the adults would have to listen. They'd have to sew up the seats of their pants and dresses. And if that didn't work, I'd blast 'em all with my stinkiest stank! We'd make them think we could smell their underpants. The kids would holler 'STINKY UNDERPANTS' at every single pair of boxers, briefs, and bloomers they saw!"

"Quick question," said Mr. Stuffington. "Don't mean to interrupt your thrilling conclusion, Stinky, but why do they call it a pair of underwear when there is only one item of clothing?"

"That is so weird," muttered Geri.

"I'm not sure," I said. "And it's not important. At least not for our story. Bob was about to go back to the city!"

"Wait a second," said Geri. "Didn't the queen want to toss Bob into her dungeon?"

"Yes, she did," I answered. "Bob knew the risks. But the children needed him. Bob and I caught the next oxcart back to the city. As we approached the city gates, the first thing we saw was the town crier. We both gasped in disbelief."

"Why?" asked Geri. "Was he still sob-bing?"

"Yes. But he also wasn't wearing any pants, ripped or otherwise. He just wore underpants!"

CHAPTER FIFTEEN

BOTTOMS UP

Now all the kids on the story rug were covering their eyes.

They were using their imaginations to picture the town crier in nothing but his tighty-whities.

It was not a pretty picture.

"The town crier told us that everybody in the city was now wearing only underwear on their bottoms. It was easier than ripping holes in their clothes. But it was almost winter. It really wasn't a good time to be running around without pants."

"So now they don't split their pants to show their underwear to the queen?" asked Geri. "They just wear underwear?"

"Exactly," I said. "It was one big Only Wear Underwear to Work Day. They still had on their fancy tops, fancy hats, and even fancier shoes and socks. But all they had on their bottoms were underpants."

"One more quick question," said Mr. Stuffington. "If underpants aren't under pants, can they still be called underpants?"

"Good question," I told him. "But Bob and I didn't have time to ask it. We sprang into action. We raced through the streets. We gathered together all the children of Wolfesburgh.

"One girl said I smelled worse than her dog's breath after he eats horse poop! I took that as a compliment."

"Um, maybe you shouldn't have," said Wags.

I ignored him.

"And so," I said, raising one paw heroically, "the brave children marched with us to the palace. The grown-ups were parading around by the gates in their underpants. The kids snaked their way through the crowd crying 'underpants!'

"But, instead of being embarrassed, the grown-ups smiled and gave their patooties a wee wiggle. They bragged about how beautiful their boxers and bloomers were.

"An elegant lady-in-waiting wore the top half of a ruffled gown and a cone-shaped hat with a veil streaming off the tip. Her underpants had the queen's face printed all over them.

"Bob turned to me. He needed help.

"So I did what needed to be done. I raised my tail and went to work. Out came one of my foulest combinations: cat barf in a dirty diaper topped with moldy green cheese!

"Bob stood on a wooden crate and called out to his troops. On his count of three, they all shouted how they smelled London, they smelled France, they smelled stinky underpants. They cried it so loudly, they shook the palace's windows. Suddenly, up on the third floor, a pair of doors flew open. The queen stepped onto her royal balcony. The crowd below grew quiet. The grown-ups closest to me also pinched their noses.

"For a moment, the queen said nothing. She just sniffed the putrid air. My stomach-churning odor had climbed all the way up to the royal balcony. Her eyes watered. She looked queasy. Finally, she made another grand pronouncement."

We are not amused.

CHAPTER SIXTEEN

THE FINAL STINKFEST

Now all the kids in the library were leaning forward. They were hanging on my every word.

"The crowd gasped," I told them. "Then more of them smelled me and wished they hadn't breathed in so deeply. The queen looked sick to her stomach.

"The adults gasped again. And, right away, they all wished they hadn't breathed in so deeply. They knew the queen was right. They all had stinky underpants!

"The queen raised both arms skyward as if she were begging for a miracle. She wished for some way for the people of Wolfesburgh to show their love without producing such an unpleasant aroma."

"Overpants!" said Abby.

"What?" said Geri.

"Overpants!" Abby explained. "Everyone should wear one pair of underpants *under* their pants. And then get another pair of underpants to wear *over* their pants! We can call that pair '*overpants*'!"

"Yes, Abby. That's exactly what Bob said. Just like you, Bob was using his

imagination! Bob quickly found Mr. William D. Wolfe in the crowd. He pitched him his idea. Mr. Wolfe loved it. He gave Bob a brand-new job. They were going into the overpants business together. Soon, Bob was the city's most famous fashion designer! He was a *superstar*—all because of his imagination!"

The library kids all applauded.

"Everybody loved their overpants," I said. "And since everybody needed to purchase two pairs of underwear—one for under their pants and one for over their pants—sales doubled over night.

"The queen was pleased. Her loyal subjects didn't stink. They also looked like superheroes. Superheroes always wear their underwear on top of their tights.

"Bob dreamed up other new product ideas for Mr. Wolfe, too. Including the Wolfe Brand Dogbrella, which kept dogs dry in the rain."

"Oh, that's such a good idea," said Wags. "I want one, I want one."

"And they all lived happily ever after?" asked Abby.

"Yes," I told her. "They did. Especially all those dogs with their new Dogbrellas."

CHAPTER SEVENTEEN

HAPPY ENDINGS

"Woo-hoo!" the kids shouted as they clapped.

"Thank you, Stinky!" said Abby.

"Thank you for coming up with that terrific ending!" I told her.

"I must admit, Stinky," said Mr. Stuffington, "you certainly know how to spin a good yarn."

"Yarn?" said Geri. "Are we going to knit mittens now?"

"No, Geri," said Mateo with a laugh. "A yarn is another word for a story."

That's when Mrs. Emerson strolled back to the story nook. We stuffies all froze.

"Children?" said Mrs. Emerson, arching an eyebrow. "What's all this fuss about?"

"We were just talking about what happened to the sheep after the boy cried 'wolf'!" said Justus.

"Yeah," said Mateo. "And stinky underpants!"

"Really?" said Mrs. Emerson, giving

me a sly look. "How . . . interesting."

"Oh, it was," said Justus.

"We hope there'll be lots more stories just like it!" said Abby.

"Well, children, this is your library," said Mrs. Emerson. "There will always be stories waiting for you here." She turned and gave me another wink. "Especially if we all use our imaginations. Isn't that right, Stinky?"

"Um, Mrs. Emerson?" said Mateo. "Stinky is a stuffed skunk. He can't hear you."

"Is that so?" said Mrs. Emerson. "Well, guess what, boys and girls? In my imagination, Stinky can do just about anything!"

Yep, just like I told you. Mrs. Emerson is the nicest person in the whole school.

Probably the smartest, too!

CHRIS GRABENSTEIN is the multiple award-winning, #1 *New York Times* bestselling author of the Mr. Lemoncello's Library, Smartest Kid in the Universe, and Dog Squad series. He's also coauthored three dozen funny books for kids with James Patterson and the acclaimed *Shine!* with his wife, J.J.

Courtesy J.J. Myers Grabenstein

J.J. MYERS GRABENSTEIN is an award-winning audiobook narrator and stage actress. She appeared in Broadway tours and starred Off-Broadway in the musical comedy *Nunsense*. She is the coauthor, with her husband, Chris Grabenstein, of the highly acclaimed middle grade novel *Shine!* J.J. and Chris live in New York City with their two cats.

ALEX PATRICK was born in the Kentish town of Dartford in the southeast of England and has been drawing for as long as he can remember.

His lifelong love for cartoons, picture books, and comics has shaped him into the passionate children's illustrator he is today. Alex loves creating original characters—he brings an element of fun and humor to each of his illustrations and is often found laughing to himself as he draws.